S0-AIJ-398

A Card for my Father

Samantha Thornhill

illustrated by Morgan Clement

penny
candy
BOOKS

Penny Candy Books
Oklahoma City & Savannah
Text © 2018 Samantha Thornhill
Illustrations © 2018 Morgan Clement

All rights reserved. Published 2018. Printed in Canada.

 This book is printed on paper certified to the environmental and social standards of the Forest Stewardship Council™ (FSC®).

Photo of Samantha Thornhill: Janelle Hamrick Photography
Design: Shanna Compton

22 21 20 19 18   1 2 3 4 5
ISBN-13: 978-0-9987999-6-4 (hardcover)

Books for the kid in *all* of us
www.pennycandybooks.com

For Angelica, Sanday & Nydesha

Flora Gardener wished Father's Day would just vanish from the calendar.

There'd be no school Daddy Day picnics and dad show-and-tells to suffer through, and definitely no card-making!

Pictures of dads and magazines littered every table in room 104. Ms. B pushed around her art cart.

Kids snatched up supplies like they were bowls of brownies with mountains of vanilla ice cream.

She spotted Jonas Borkholder nearby sinking into his chair, too. But Bork was the class hermit who always slouched.

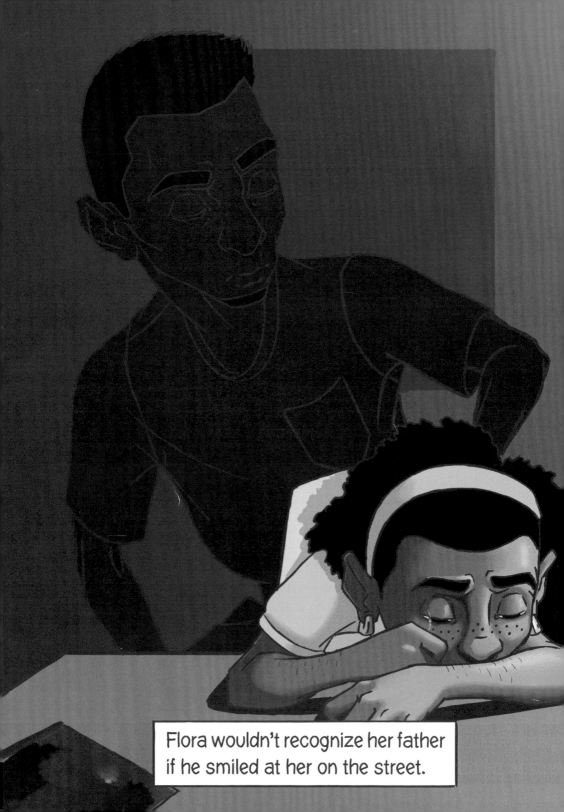

Flora wouldn't recognize her father if he smiled at her on the street.

Ever since Flora could remember, her mother would suddenly lose her hearing when asked about *him*, the man who gave Flora such dark arm hairs and eyes.

When Flora was four, she decided that she would find her father without her mother's help or knowing.

One Sunday, Flora was certain of her father.

At high mass, she ran up to the altar during Father Francis's sermon, hugged the priest's robed knees and shouted,

Before she could utter another word, her mother plucked her out of that cathedral like a silent tornado.

Since then, a faceless man has ghosted across Flora's dreams. Even the good ones.

"Did you bring
a daddy picture, Flora?"
Ms. B asked.

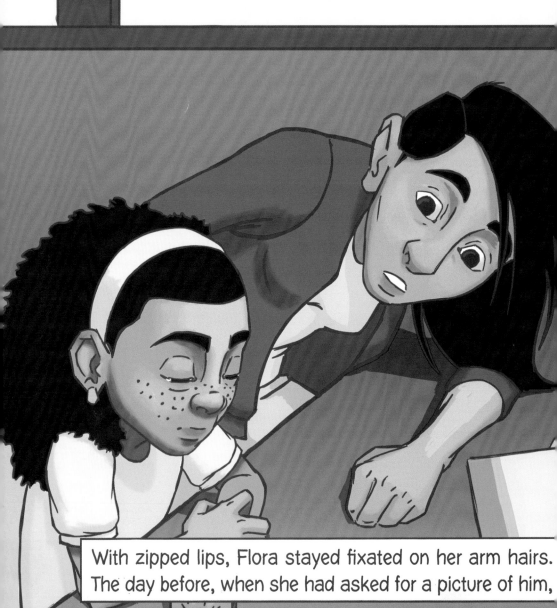

With zipped lips, Flora stayed fixated on her arm hairs.
The day before, when she had asked for a picture of him,

her mother's eyes filled up like storm clouds that never rained, and that was the end of that.

What to do?

Flora wanted to hide inside the cover's glossy sunflower field until Father's Day was over.

Show and tell wasn't so bad—at first.
Melissa's father was a firefighter.

Bobby's father was sitting in a cockpit. Flora could almost see herself soaring through clouds with Captain Dad.

Then when she remembered her own faceless phantom, she soon felt like an eel at the bottom of the sea.

Before her classmates closed in like sharks, Flora took up her scissors and sliced into a magazine, pretending to be deaf.

After school, she spotted Bork still hunched over his card, and peeked.

"Why are you making a
Father's Day card for the
President??"
she blurted.

Bork looked directly at her for the first time.
His eyes were the blue of swimming pools.

"My dad's dead. And the president
is sort of everybody's dad,"
he answered, matter-of-factly.

"Did you finish your card?"

"My mom's here,"
she said, relieved to keep
her secret.

The next morning, Flora started coughing when her mother breezed into her bedroom and opened the curtains.

"I think I'm allergic to
school today,"
    Flora croaked.

        "Sorry, kiddo, I can't
    take any more days off,"
            her mom said.

Flora sulked all the way to school. Class was too festive over Daddy Day picnic to notice the cloud of sadness she was.

Ms. B called her over.

"Today, you can picnic with me on my special blanket. It's for people like us, whose fathers can't be here today," she said.

Flora trudged to her table. Her sadness followed her like her very own shadow, like the faceless man in her dreams...

...all the way to the picnic, to the bright island of Ms. B's blanket. There she sat, watching dads trickle into the park wearing work outfits and smiles.

One by one kids ran to greet them with hugs, kisses, and cards.

Then, she noticed an all too familiar face. The most beautiful face in all the world. Flora flew into her arms.

"Is this for me?"

She pinched the card from Flora's hand and stared, mesmerized by the collage within.

A familiar wrinkle appeared between her eyebrows before smoothing again.

Flora summoned every crumb of courage within her to ask...

"If I send it to him, do you think he'll write me back?"

Her mother looked past her, like she was looking across town, or into another time. Flora's heart quickened.

She held her breath. In a tiny corner of her imagination, her faceless father started to take shape as he walked toward her from whatever distant place he was in.

Her mother
answered,

"There's only one
way to find out."

Stay tuned for Book 2 in this series

The Job My Dad Never Leaves

Samantha Thornhill is a poet, educator, producer, and author of three children's books, including the poem in *Odetta: The Queen of Folk*. Her work has been published in over two-dozen literary journals and anthologies, such as *The BreakBeat Poets: New American Poetry in the Age of Hip-Hop*. A performer on stages across the United States and internationally, she holds an MFA from the University of Virginia. For ten years, Samantha lived in Brooklyn where she taught poetry to acting students at the Juilliard School. She also served as a writer-in-residence at the Bronx Academy of Letters, where she taught creative writing seminars to youth. A cofounder of Poets in Unexpected Places, which was profiled in the *New York Times* for their surprising pop-up poetry experiments all over New York City, Samantha also facilitates workshops for the Dialogue Arts Project, which ventures into professional settings and uses creative writing as a tool to navigate uncomfortable discussions about social identity. Samantha is a native of the twin island nation of Trinidad and Tobago. To learn more about Samantha and her works visit www.samanthaspeaks.com.

Morgan Clement was born in Atlanta, Georgia, and raised in Cleveland, Ohio. She always loved to draw as a child but didn't consider it to be a serious career option until high school when she attended a college preview program at the Columbus College of Art & Design in Columbus, Ohio. After graduating from high school, Morgan went on to pursue a Bachelor of Fine Arts in Animation at the Savannah College of Art & Design in Savannah, Georgia. Through SCAD she was able to expand her skills and even got the opportunity to study abroad at SCAD's Hong Kong campus, studying both painting and illustration. She works as a freelance graphic designer and illustrator and loves to work on comic books and other forms of sequential art.

Thank you, Zac Murphy, for your immense support. Big ups to Kyle Dargan, Lauren Alleyne, Quraysh Ali Lansana, and Al Malnik, as well as the Furious Flower Poetry Center at James Madison University, for making the publication and completion of this book possible. My family.

—Samantha